Rock-a-Doodle-Do!

Michael Foreman

an adaptation of a tale by the Brothers Grimm

Andersen Press
London

Not long ago, there was this old donkey. He had worked hard all his life but, now that he was not as strong as he had been, his master wanted to get rid of him.

Now, the donkey didn't want to be made into pet food, so he decided to run away to the city and fulfil his dream of becoming a musician.

Copyright © 2000 by Michael Foreman
The rights of Michael Foreman to be identified as the author and illustrator
of this adaptation of *The Musicians of Bremen* by the Brothers Grimm have been asserted
by him in accordance with the Copyright, Designs and Patents Act, 1988.
First published in Great Britain in 2000 by Andersen Press Ltd.,
20 Vauxhall Bridge Road, London SW1V 2SA. Published in Australia by
Random House Australia Pty., 20 Alfred Street, Milsons Point, Sydney, NSW 2061.
All rights reserved. Colour separated in Switzerland by Photolitho AG, Zürich.
Printed and bound in Italy by Grafiche AZ, Verona.

10   9   8   7   6   5   4   3   2   1

British Library Cataloguing in Publication Data available.

ISBN 0 86264 951 X

This book has been printed on acid-free paper

Off he went down the road with a
"Hee-haw, Hee-haw".

Soon he met an old dog panting by the roadside.
"Now then, Rover. Why so huffy and puffy?"

"Oh!" gasped the dog. "Just because I can't hunt rabbits anymore, my master thinks I'm not worth my keep and wants to get rid of me. What will become of me now, I don't know."

"Why don't you come with me?" asked the donkey. "We'll be musicians together."

So, off they went down the road with a "Hee-haw, Hee-haw, Woof, Woof, Woof".

Just around the next bend, they found a cat
sitting in the middle of the road
with a face as long as a fiddle.
    "Why so sad, old Sour Puss?"
asked the donkey.

"Oh!" sighed the cat. "Just because I am old and like sitting by the fire instead of chasing mice, my mistress thinks I'm not worth my keep and wants to drown me. I've escaped so far, but I don't know where to go."

"All cats like serenading," said the donkey. "Come with us to the big city and join our band."

So, off they went down the road with a "Hee-haw, Hee-haw, Woof, Woof, Miaow".

Soon they came to a farm and there, sitting on a fence, was a rooster, crowing fit to burst.

"Hush, my friend," said the donkey. "Why are you crowing as if there will be no tomorrow?"

"Because there *will be* no tomorrow!" cried the rooster.
"The farmer's wife says I'm going in the pot tonight.
I'm singing my song while I have the chance."

"Bring your song to the city. We'll make
fine use of it there," said the donkey.

So, off they went down the road
with a "Hee-haw, Hee-haw,
Woof, Woof, Miaow, Miaow,

Rock-a-doodle-do!"

But the city was further than they thought.
By evening they were at the edge of a wood
and decided to stay there for the night.
The donkey and the dog lay down
under a broad tree, and the cat and
the cock went up into the branches.

Before he went to sleep, the cock had a final look
around, and saw a faint glimmer of light in the distance.

"A light!" he crowed. "I see a light! There might be
a house, and food."

"Very well," sighed the donkey. "Let's all get up and
go on a bit further. It's not very comfy here."

So, off they set again with a "Hee-haw, Woof, Miaow,
Rock-a-doodle . . . Yawn!"

As they got closer, they saw that the light came from an old roadside café.

"Yummy," said the dog, licking his chops. "A café, of all places."

"We haven't any money," whined old Sour Puss. "And anyway, it looks closed."

The donkey was tall enough to peer in through the window.

"Uh, oh!" he whispered. "It's worse than closed. It's full of robbers."

"What?!" they gasped.

The dog jumped on the donkey's back to take a look. The cat jumped on the dog's back and the cock flew up onto the cat's head.

With a crash the old window gave way and they all fell
into the café in a shower of broken glass.
  The donkey yelled, the dog howled, the cat
screeched and the cock crowed.
The robbers threw up their arms
and fled in a panic, leaving
their dinner and the money
behind them.

The animals looked at the table.
"Could be worse," grinned the dog.
"Couldn't be better," purred old Sour Puss.

After finishing the best meal they had ever eaten,
the four friends found comfortable places to sleep.

The donkey, who liked country air, slept on the porch, the dog behind the door, the cat in the warmth of the kitchen, and the cock put out the light and flew up into the rafters. They were soon asleep.

But the robbers hadn't gone far.
"We can't leave all that loot behind!"
said the boss, and when they
saw the light go out he
sent one of his men back
to the café to see what
was happening.

The robber found everything quiet! He climbed
in through the kitchen window – and trod on the cat.
The cat flew at his face, spitting and scratching.
  Terrified, the robber ran out of the kitchen and
tripped over the dog who bit him in the leg.
The cock pecked at the robber's head and
the donkey gave him a tremendous kick
in the pants which sent him flying.

When the rest of the gang saw the robber
limping back, covered in lumps and bumps,
they gave up all hope of getting the money back,
and vanished into the night.

So, the four friends never went to the city.

They didn't need to. The city came to them . . .

With a "Rock-a-doodle-do . . .